To my son, Hunter. You will always
be important to me and Daddy.

WWW.MASCOTBOOKS.COM

Paws and Think!™: I Am Important

For more information, please contact:
Mascot Books
560 Herndon Parkway #120
Herndon, VA 20170
info@mascotbooks.com

CPSIA Code: PBANG0717A
Library of Congress Control Number: 2017907829
ISBN-13: 978-1-68401-264-0

Printed in the United States

PAWS and THINK!™

I AM IMPORTANT

MIRANDA MITTLEMAN

ILLUSTRATED BY INDOS STUDIOS

I see other dogs all of the time,
But their lives are all very different from mine.

POLICE

They have lots
of important jobs to do,

Police dogs, guide dogs,
and dogs on TV too!

But am I important? Why am I here?

Will anyone miss me if I disappear?

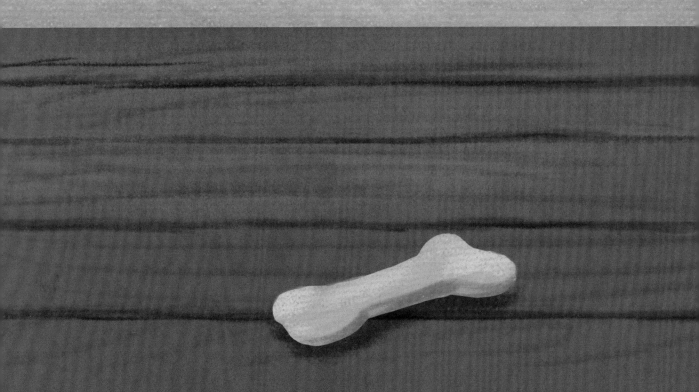

So I dug a hole under my fence and I ran away.

Maybe I'll be someone important today!

I looked down the streets
and in the park,

I tried to find a job
before it got dark.

LOST DOG

CALL 555-1234

But as I explored the city,
what did I see?

Posters everywhere
with a picture of me!

My family already knew
I was gone,

They must have seen me missing
from our tiny lawn!

So I came back home
and saw Mommy crying,

And heard Daddy say,
"We'll find him! Let's keep trying!"

That's when I realized
I have a great job to do,

I make my family happy
and that's important too!

So the next time you wonder
but can't quite tell,

PAWS and THINK!
You are important as well!

Miranda Mittleman grew up in Baltimore, Maryland, where she earned her bachelor's degree in marketing from Towson University. She's an avid runner, has a black belt in karate, and was even a contestant on *Wheel of Fortune!* But her true passion has always been poetry. She can recite most poems from her childhood by heart and was inspired to write the ***PAWS and THINK!***™ series while living in the city with her husband, Michael, and their playful mutt, Weaver.

Have a book idea?

Contact us at:

560 Herndon Parkway
Suite 120
Herndon, VA 20170
info@mascotbooks.com | www.mascotbooks.com

See what lesson I dig up next!